Garfield's PET FORCE®

BOOK 5
ATTACK OF THE LETHAL LIZARDS

Other titles in this series:

Garfield's Pet Force #1:
The Outrageous Origin

Garfield's Pet Force #2:
Pie-Rat's Revenge!

Garfield's Pet Force #3:
K-Niner—Dog of Doom!

Garfield's Pet Force #4:
Menace of the Mutanator!

Visit Garfield's Pet Force at
www.garfield.com/petforce

Visit Scholastic's Web site at
www.scholastic.com

Produced by Creative Media Applications, Inc., and Paws Incorporated
Interior Graphics by Tom Howard and Jeff Wesley

ISBN 0-439-11092-0

12 11 10 9 8 7 6 5 4 3 2 1   9/9 0 1 2 3 4/0

Printed in the U.S.A.   40

First Scholastic printing, September 1999

Garfield's PET FORCE®

BOOK 5
ATTACK OF THE LETHAL LIZARDS

Created by
Jim Davis

Character development by
Mark Acey & Gary Barker

Written by
Michael Teitelbaum

Illustrated by
Gary Barker & Larry Fentz

SCHOLASTIC INC.
New York Toronto London Auckland Sydney
Mexico City New Delhi Hong Kong

Introduction

When a group of lovable pets — Garfield, Odie, Arlene, Nermal, and Pooky — are transported to an alternate universe, they become a mighty superhero team known as . . . *Pet Force*!

Garzooka — Large and in charge, he is the fearless and famished leader of Pet Force. He's a ferocious feline with nerves of steel, a razor-sharp right claw, and the awesome ability to fire gamma-radiated hairballs (as well as deadly one-liners) from his mouth.

Odious — Although utterly clueless, he possesses incredible strength, ultra-slippery slobber, and a super-stretchy stun tongue. One zap of his lethal wet tongue causes a total mental meltdown in anyone he unleashes it upon.

Starlena — Sings a *purrfectly* pitched siren song ("the meow that wows!"). Anyone who hears her hypnotic song immediately falls into a trance — except Garzooka.

Abnermal — Has a body temperature of absolute zero; one touch of his icy paw freezes foes in their tracks. He can extend a nuke-proof force field to protect himself, as well as the other Pet Force members. His pester-power — more annoying than your little brother! — is one power that Garzooka could live without.

Compooky — Part-computer, part-teddy, this cyberbear extraordinaire is not only incredibly cute, but is also the mental giant of the team (not that big a deal).

Behold the mighty Pet Force! *Let the fur fly!*

1

The story so far . . .

There are a great many universes parallel to our own. Each of these universes is very much like ours, but each one differs in some way. For example, in our universe Jon Arbuckle is a nice but dim-witted pet owner. In the particular parallel universe that concerns our story, Jon is a nice but dim-witted emperor. In our universe, Garfield, Odie, Nermal, and Arlene are pets, and Pooky is a teddy bear. When these five friends travel into the parallel universe ruled by Emperor Jon, they become superpowered heroes.

In each universe there is a dimensional portal, a doorway that connects one world to another. When danger strikes in Emperor Jon's universe, the emperor summons Garfield, Odie, Nermal, Arlene, and Pooky, who pass through the dimensional doorway from our universe into that of Emperor Jon.

In our universe, the doorway is the cover of issue #100 of the *Pet Force* comic book. When that framed comic book cover — which hangs on the wall in Jon Arbuckle's living room — begins to glow, the doorway to the other universe opens and the pets are pulled into the cover.

In Emperor Jon's universe, the doorway is a large magic cauldron that belongs to the emperor's trusted friend and adviser, Sorcerer Binky. When the five friends arrive in Emperor Jon's universe, they emerge from this magic cauldron, transformed into the superpowered heroes of Pet Force. The same thing is true in reverse: When it is time for the five to go home, they pass through the cauldron and come back out of the comic book cover into their own universe, where they are no longer superheroes.

Because time passes differently in the two universes, Garfield and his friends could be in the parallel universe for days or weeks, while only seconds pass in our universe. Jon never misses his pets, and he certainly doesn't suspect they could be superheroes in another universe! The fact that his brain runs a few minutes behind the rest of the world doesn't hurt, either!

When trouble arises in Emperor Jon's universe, it is usually caused by Vetvix, an evil veterinarian. Using evil spells and dark magic, she has vowed to conquer the universe and take the crown from good Emperor Jon.

2

Vetvix's schemes to conquer Emperor Jon's universe would succeed if not for the power of Pet Force — those five, furry defenders of justice who have stopped her again and again.

At the moment, things are calm and peaceful in Emperor Jon's universe. Pet Force has defeated all of Vetvix's dangerous henchmen. As for Vetvix herself, she is trapped aboard her orbiting headquarters, known as the *Floating Fortress of Fear*. And she is not feeling like herself. In her last battle with Pet Force, Vetvix was split apart by her own combination machine. As of now, Vetvix's arms are attached to a cow, her legs are attached to a gerbil, and her body is attached to a cheetah's head. Her head is attached to a lizard's body, which is locked in a force field prison on her

Fortress. And with her body split apart, Vetvix has lost her magical powers.

With Vetvix trapped, the members of Pet Force are in our universe, the one containing the Earth we all know and love, being regular pets. And they are certain Emperor Jon's crown is safe.

And so, for the time being, things are quiet in the universe of Emperor Jon. But as you well know, dear reader, nothing stays quiet around there for very long!

2

Our universe, Jon Arbuckle's living room . . .

"I got them! I got them!" shouted Jon Arbuckle, racing from his mailbox into his house.

"What did he get now?" moaned Garfield. "More books on the pleasures of wearing plaid? Or maybe it's videos of *Here Come the Nerds, Parts XI* and *XII*." Garfield was lying on the living room rug like a big orange throw pillow. Near his head, a timer ticked away. *Ding!* The timer rang, indicating that it was time for Garfield to stop napping on his left side.

"The tickets are here!" exclaimed Jon, jumping around the living room as if the carpet were on fire. "Our plane tickets and passes to WackyWorld are here! Vacation, here we come!"

Jon planned to take the gang on a vacation to the WackyWorld theme park. The park was based on Jon's favorite television cartoon characters, the

Wackys — Willie and Wanda Wacky, and their wacky kids, Wilma, Wendell, and Wally.

"*The Wackys* is kind of a dumb show," Nermal said to Garfield as the bigger cat rolled over onto his right side.

"Right up your alley, then," replied Garfield, resetting his timer, then cuddling up with Pooky.

"I think it's a funny show," said Arlene. "And I for one am very excited about taking a real vacation. I know Odie's excited, too."

Garfield glanced over to see Odie chewing on the TV remote. Small sparks flew from the unit as drool oozed under the buttons. It frizzled and frazzled, then died with a crackling sound.

"Oh, great. Now we can't even change channels," groaned Garfield. "We'll be forced to watch nothing but Jon's favorite channel, the Miniature Golf Network. Twenty-four hours of windmills, clowns, and whining brats smacking the ball into the parking lot."

"Well, gang," said Jon, looking over the tickets for the tenth time. "We leave in two days, so I'd better get packing. I wonder what clothes to bring?" Jon bounded upstairs to his bedroom, still clutching the tickets tightly in his hand.

"Let me guess," said Garfield. "Plaid. All plaid."

Emperor Jon's universe, the planet Reptilius . . .

There was nothing particularly special about the planet Reptilius. It was located in a far corner of Emperor Jon's universe. Steamy jungles covered most of the planet. Swamps, rivers, and lakes dotted the landscape. Reptilius's tropical environment had led to the development of many types of reptiles. Snakes, lizards, turtles, and crocodiles made up the entire population of the small planet.

Reptilius was not a remarkable planet, but something truly bizarre was happening there. Miles and miles above the planet's surface, Vetvix's *Floating Fortress of Fear* orbited the jungle world. The evil veterinarian, Pet Force's archenemy, had built her *Fortress* in space above Reptilius quite by chance. At the moment, Vetvix was imprisoned within the *Fortress* and knew nothing about the happenings on Reptilius. But her evil was still creating havoc in the universe.

Over the past few months, during Vetvix's experiments with K-Niner and the Mutanator (see Pet Force Books #3 and #4), a tremendous amount of magical energy had been radiating from the *Floating Fortress*. Because of the angle from the *Fortress* to the planet's surface, one particular swamp on Reptilius had been bombarded with most of this magical energy. The energy affected all the inhabitants of that swamp to some degree.

7

But three creatures in particular had been undergoing an astounding transformation that was about to be completed.

A fifteen-foot-long snake burst from the thick jungle brush. Just weeks ago, he had been only eleven inches long and had no fangs. Now, thanks to the magical energy from Vetvix's *Fortress*, he had not only grown to enormous length and sprouted deadly, venom-filled fangs, but he could also think and talk.

"What has happened to me?" he said aloud. "I'm big. Really big! And I've got fangs, too! What has happened to me?"

"Probably the same thing that has happened to me," replied a shrill voice.

The snake whipped his scaly head around and bared his fangs. He was face-to-face with a chameleon. But this was no ordinary chameleon.

Like the snake, the chameleon had been transformed by the magical energy blasting the planet. He now stood on his hind legs, over five feet tall, his long tail lashing behind him. Just like when he was small, his eyes rotated independently, giving him the power to look in two directions at once. Now his tongue darted swiftly from his mouth, striking the snake straight between his eyes.

The snake was stunned silly for a moment. Then he reacted quickly. He whipped his enormous body around the chameleon and began to squeeze.

8

The snake's powerful muscles contracted and the chameleon felt his ribs about to snap.

Suddenly, the chameleon's body transformed. Within seconds, he had changed his appearance. Now he looked exactly like the snake. He tangled himself up with the snake so completely that the snake wasn't sure whether he was squeezing himself or his opponent.

"Huh?" said the snake. "How did you do that?"

The chameleon's body shape changed again, this time into a tiny bird that flew to a nearby branch. Then he changed back into his chameleon form and hopped down to the ground. "It seems that I can now change my form simply by thinking of whatever I want to look like," the chameleon realized. "This could prove to be a very useful power!"

"Do the bird thing again," said the snake, knowing that this creature would make a better ally than an enemy. "I liked the bird thing."

Before either of them could move, a wall of bright orange flame tore through the jungle, singeing them both. "It appears I am not alone in my magnificent transformation," boomed a voice from the jungle. "However, I declare myself leader of this little group."

A huge Komodo dragon, standing over ten feet tall, burst from the dense jungle foliage. He stopped in front of the snake and the chameleon. The dragon's body rippled with muscles. A protective armor ran from his massive shoulders to the top of his head. Long, sharp claws gleamed from both his back and front legs. A wicked-looking, three-foot tail whipped back and forth behind him. He sent another stream of fire shooting from his mouth, causing the other two lizards to dive for cover.

"What makes you think you should be the leader?" asked the chameleon as he got to his feet.

"Well, let's see — my superior brains, my incredible strength, my sharp claws, and my newfound ability to breath fire," replied Dragon. "That and the fact that I could kick your chameleon tush from here to the next swamp."

"Oh, yeah?" cried Chameleon, tensing his body and charging toward Dragon. "You and what army?" Chameleon lashed out with his dynamic, darting tongue as he ran.

Dragon reached out, grabbed Chameleon's tongue, and yanked. Chameleon went sailing into a tree. "My army, wise guy!" Dragon shouted at Chameleon. "My army of one! Me!"

Not wanting to be left out of the power struggle, Snake attacked Dragon from behind. He wrapped his powerful, fifteen-foot-long body around Dragon's chest, then moved his poisonous fangs toward Dragon's head. Dragon caught Snake's neck in his powerful fist, stopping the deadly fangs. Snake's air supply was cut off. He released his grip on Dragon, who then sent Snake flying with a powerful punch.

"I'm coming, Mom!" muttered a stunned and confused Snake as he hit the ground with a *thud*. "I'll set the table for dinner!"

Dragon turned back to Chameleon, who had just gotten to his feet. Dragon slashed at his opponent with his supersharp claws.

Chameleon instantly changed into a tiny salamander to avoid Dragon's vicious claws. He then disappeared into the dense undergrowth of the jungle floor.

"That's right, coward, run away!" snarled Dragon. What he didn't know was that Chameleon had raced a short distance, transformed himself into a huge rhinoceros, and was now charging at Dragon's back.

Dragon heard the thundering of the rhino. "What?" he blurted out as he turned around, just in time to take the full impact of the rhino's charge in his chest. Dragon's back slammed into a thick-trunked tree.

"It's time for you to start calling *me* 'Boss,' Boss," shouted Chameleon. He closed in for a second devastating blow.

"Is that before or after I turn you into a well-done rhino burger?" snarled Dragon, blasting Chameleon with a burst of fiery breath.

Chameleon felt his rhino skin burning. *Got to change back, before it's too late!* he thought as he reverted to his normal chameleon form. The painful burning stopped, but he collapsed in an exhausted heap at Dragon's feet. "Okay," Chameleon muttered. "You win. You're the boss." *For now*, he thought.

Snake slithered up beside the others. "Is dinner ready yet, Mom?" he asked, still dazed and confused from his encounter with Dragon.

Dragon grabbed Snake's head and shook it like a rattle.

"Oh, it's you, Boss!" Snake said, snapping to attention. "I was having the weirdest dream."

"We've got to figure out what happened to us," announced Dragon as he led the others deeper into the jungle. "One day we're normal lizards, happily crawling around the swamp —"

"Some of us were slithering, not crawling," interrupted Snake. "I just wanted to make that point."

"— and the next day, we've all grown in size, and we can think and speak," finished Dragon, giving Snake a dirty look.

"I say, who cares how we got this way?" said Chameleon as the group made their way across a narrow river. "We've got great powers here. Let's use them. We should be running this place."

Before Dragon could respond, a pack of fierce, hungry crocodiles attacked the band of lizards. The river was alive with the thrashing tails and snapping jaws of the vicious crocs.

Chameleon reacted first, firing his dynamic, darting tongue at a croc, which was knocked from the river by the tongue's force. Snake sank his fangs into the soft, white throat of another croc, injecting his venom. That croc collapsed, motion-

13

less. Dragon, meanwhile, was grabbing one croc after another with his powerful arms and tossing them from the river. They scattered off into the jungle. Within seconds, the battle was over.

"We're quite a team for a bunch of lowly lizards," said Snake proudly.

"We are not just normal lizards!" Dragon shouted, raising his fists into the air, bursting with excitement at his newfound power. "From now on we shall be known as the *Lethal Lizards*!"

3

Emperor Jon's universe . . .

"**N**ow where did I put that mask and snorkel?" asked Emperor Jon as he frantically searched through a closet in his throne room.

With things in his universe quiet for the first time in a while, Emperor Jon had seized the opportunity to take a long-awaited vacation. Pet Force had set things right, Vetvix was trapped in a prison of her own making, and the emperor had finally finished cataloging his collection of shower curtain liners. With this important work done, he was free to leave his castle on the planet Polyester. At the moment, the emperor was packing his bags for a trip to Funlandia, the most popular vacation planet in his universe.

Binky the Sorcerer, the emperor's trusted friend and adviser, was helping him pack. The sorcerer would be in charge of the palace while the emperor was away.

"O great Emperor," began Sorcerer Binky. "Your mask and snorkel are —"

"No, don't tell me," interrupted the emperor. "I just saw them a minute ago. They've got to be in here somewhere." Jon dug deeper, tossing items out over his shoulders as he pawed through the huge

pile of junk in his closet. Orange, hightop sneakers, plaid slacks, ancient copies of *Emperor's Life* magazine, a single roller skate, an old accordion, a gallon jar of mayonnaise, and a half-eaten corned beef sandwich went zipping past the sorcerer's head.

"But, Your Highness, I —" Binky tried again, ducking out of the way of the flying objects.

"Look at this!" shouted Jon, emerging from the closet waving an unpaid electric bill in his hand. "That's where this went. No wonder they turned the power off here at the palace. And all this time, we've been using candles." Then he dove back in.

"Emperor Jon," said the sorcerer. He got no response. "Emperor Jon!" he said a little louder. Still no reaction from the emperor, who was digging furiously through the mounds of junk.

"EMPEROR JON!" Binky finally shouted, using his magically enhanced, super-loud voice.

This finally got the emperor's attention. The force of the shout knocked the emperor into the back wall of his closet. Swimming through the mess, the emperor came out from the closet, quite annoyed. "I've asked you before not to use your super-loud voice," said the emperor. "Now, what could be so important that you have

to pull me away from my search for my mask and snorkel?"

"Your Highness," began the sorcerer, his voice returning to a normal volume, "your mask and snorkel are on your head. You tried them on this morning and forgot to pack them."

Jon reached up and felt the mask that was strapped tightly over his eyes and nose. His snorkel bobbed from a plastic strap attached to the mask. "No wonder things in my closet looked a little cloudy. I thought that was just because I haven't cleaned in a while."

"A couple of decades," muttered Binky.

"Well," said Jon, pulling the mask and snorkel off his head and tossing them into his suitcase. "I guess we solved that mystery."

Sorcerer Binky just sighed.

Emperor Jon was soon ready to leave. He had a duffel bag slung over each shoulder and another around his neck. He carried a suitcase in each hand. On his head rested a cap, sent to him by the Funlandia Tourist Board, which read "Ask me where I'm going."

"Go ahead, ask me," insisted Emperor Jon.

"But Your Highness, I've asked you six times today already," replied an obviously frustrated Binky.

"Come on," pleaded Jon. "Ask me one more time."

"Very well," said Binky. "Where are you going?"

"To Fun-Fun-Funlandia!" shouted Jon, repeating the vacation planet's slogan. "The land of fundia! For fun-fun-fun!" Then he burst into laughter.

Binky smiled politely, then helped the emperor out of the palace and over to the shuttle, which was waiting to whisk him off to Funlandia.

"Now remember," said the emperor as he climbed aboard the small spacecraft. "While I'm gone, don't talk to strangers and don't start any wars. But feel free to use the palace as if it were your home. Also, you can wear any of my clothes you like."

Sorcerer Binky looked over the emperor's outfit of plaid pants, a checked shirt, striped sneakers, and a scarf with little smiley faces all over it. "Thanks," he muttered. "I think I'll stick with my sorcerer's robes. Have a good trip, Your Highness."

As the door to the shuttle slid closed, Sorcerer Binky could hear Jon saying to the ship's pilot, "Ask me where I'm going! Come on!" Then the ship fired up its engines and blasted off. Within seconds, it disappeared from view.

Sorcerer Binky shook his head, sighed deeply, then turned and strolled back into the palace.

The planet Funlandia was truly an amazing place. The ultimate vacation destination in the universe, it featured beautiful beaches for swimming, snorkeling, or just hanging out. Everywhere you turned, there was a golf course. And the tourist attractions and amusement parks brought travelers both young and old to this popular spot.

Emperor Jon bolted from his shuttle as soon as it landed on Funlandia. "Fun-Fun-Funlandia!" he shouted. He raced to the bus waiting to take him and other tourists to all the hot spots listed in the Funlandia brochure. The emperor had left his crown and robes at home on purpose — he did not want to receive any special treatment. He wanted to have the same type of vacation as millions of other tourists, free from the burdens of royalty and the responsibilities of ruling.

"Does this bus go to the Universe's Largest Ball of String?" asked the emperor as he climbed aboard.

"It's our first stop," replied the driver as the doors slammed shut and the bus zoomed away.

"I'm so excited about seeing it," said Emperor Jon. "I have a pretty good-sized string collection back home, but from what I read in the brochure, this ball of string is really big!"

The driver smiled politely. "That's why they call it 'the Universe's Largest Ball of String,'" he said. *I can't believe I'm having this conversation*, is what he thought.

At stop after stop, Jon *oohed* and *ahhed*, and snapped picture after picture. "Wait until Sorcerer Binky sees these shots," he said to himself. "He's going to love this stuff!"

The tour stopped next at the statue of Elias J. Topbottom, the man who invented plaid. A tear came to the emporer's eye as he stared up at the twelve-foot-tall marble sculpture, then looked down at his own plaid pants, and then looked back up at the statue. "My hero!" he exclaimed to the crowd of strangers, wiping the tear away.

The others in the crowd slowly backed away from Jon.

"Well, plaid *is* my favorite color," he explained. The others kept moving, backing toward the tour bus.

"All aboard!" shouted the bus driver. "Next stop, the Museum of Lint!"

"Wow!" exclaimed Emperor Jon as he raced to the bus. "Now that place sounds really, really interesting!"

4

Our universe, WackyWorld theme park . . .

"**O**h, boy!" exclaimed Jon as he, Odie, Arlene, Nermal, and Garfield, with Pooky at his side, passed through the enormous front gates of the WackyWorld theme park. "I feel like one of the Wackys on the TV show."

So why is this different than any other day? wondered Garfield.

Just then, an actor dressed in a Willie Wacky costume, complete with a big, round head, stepped up to the group. "Welcome to WackyWorld!" he chirped.

"No, wait a minute, don't tell me," said Jon. "You're Willie Wacky!" Jon jumped up and down with excitement.

"Yeah, you got it, mister," said Willie Wacky. "Now you want to do something about your dog?"

Odie stood next to Willie Wacky, drooling all

over his cheap costume. The annoyed actor squished as he moved.

"Oh, that's just Odie," explained Jon. "He loves your show!"

"Yeah, great, great," muttered the actor as he began to wring out his sopping wet costume. "A dog loves the show."

"He's not very friendly," said Arlene, turning to Garfield, "for a cartoon character." But Garfield was gone. "Nermal, where's Garfield?" she asked, looking around. There was no sign of Nermal, either. *Where could they have gone?* she thought.

Garfield had discovered the park's attraction that appealed to him most. It wasn't Willie Wacky's Wonderful Wagon. It wasn't Wilma Wacky's World of Worms. And it wasn't Wally Wacky's Winding Waterfall. Garfield was now stretched out on the counter of the closest Wacky-World food concession stand.

"Food," mumbled Garfield as he stuffed three WackyBurgers into his mouth. "The theme that unites all theme parks." He proceeded to eat five WackyWaffles, six DopeyDogs, twelve Peculiar-Pizzas, and a LaughableLasagna for dessert.

Then he rolled over and fell into a blissful nap. *I love vacations*, he thought, just before he drifted off.

Meanwhile, Nermal was looking at what he was most interested in — souvenir toys based on the Wackys' TV show. By the time Jon and Arlene had found him, Nermal had his arms full of Wacky merchandise. "I want the giant Wendell Wacky walking, talking, wisecracking, stuffed action figure with the automatic high-fiving right arm!" Nermal shouted. "I also want the Wilma Wacky Wild-and-Woolly board game and the Wally Wacky Wacky Pack, filled with wacky fun!"

"Come on, Nermal," said Arlene. "Let's go on some of the rides. Maybe we can get toys later."

"But I want the Wonderful Wacky Wet and Wild —"

"Later, Nermal," said Arlene. "Now where's Garfield?"

By the time they found Garfield, he had cleaned out three concession stands and was being carried away from a fourth by an angry Wanda Wacky. "Is this your cat?" she asked through her big-head costume.

Say no, say no, say no! thought Garfield, shaking his head violently.

"Yes," replied Jon.

Wanda Wacky let go of Garfield. He collapsed to the ground in a fat, furry heap. "Have a great time in WackyWorld," said Wanda. "And keep this big, orange eating machine away from the food. There *are* other visitors here, you know."

"Nice going, blimp-boy," said Arlene. "Thinking with your stomach, once again."

"Is that Wilma Wacky?" asked Garfield sarcastically, looking right at Arlene. "Oh, it's just Arlene. You could see where it would be easy to get confused. The big head, the big mouth, you know . . ."

"Come on, everyone," said Jon excitedly now that the group was reunited. "I don't want to be late for Willie Wacky's World of Walnuts. The next ride begins in five minutes. I want to be sure to ride in the front walnut!"

"Great," muttered Garfield. "A cheesy ride in a cheesy theme park with Jon, the king of cheesiness. Great vacation. And besides, all this talk of cheese has made me hungry. Anybody got any cheese?"

Nobody answered. Garfield reluctantly trudged off with the others toward the ride.

5

**Emperor Jon's universe, the planet
Reptilius . . .**

The Lethal Lizards made their way through
the dense jungle of Reptilius.

"Are we just going to spend the rest of our lives
crushing crocodiles and beating up iguanas here
on this dump?" asked Chameleon, who was
grumpy after miles and miles of plowing through
the jungle. "I think we were meant for bigger
things. Why else would we have been given these
amazing powers?"

"You know, he has a point, Boss," agreed Snake,
smiling at Dragon.

Dragon grabbed Chameleon by the throat with
one powerful hand and lifted him high into the air.

"You make a good point, too, Boss," said Snake
hastily.

"I'm the boss," Dragon snarled at Chameleon.

"I make the decisions around here." Then he dropped Chameleon to the ground.

"All right, Mr. Boss," said Chameleon sarcastically, rubbing his sore neck. "What's your plan?"

"That!" exclaimed Dragon, pointing straight ahead. The group stepped into a clearing near a marsh. "That, if I'm not mistaken, is my plan!"

In the center of the clearing sat a gleaming silver spaceship.

"What is it?" asked Snake.

"I'm not sure," replied Dragon. "But I have a feeling it's very important."

The Lethal Lizards rushed to the ship. After exploring the outside for a few minutes, Dragon found the lever that controlled the hatch. Popping it open, the three lizards scrambled inside. Dragon sat in the pilot's seat. Chameleon slipped into the copilot's seat next to him. Snake slithered behind them, with his head poking into the cockpit between the other two. The small ship was cramped, but the lizards were too excited to notice.

"Look at all the buttons and switches!" said Snake. "What's this one do?" He leaned over to the control panel and punched a button with his fang.

The ship began to shake and hum. Lights came on, and the lizards felt a surge of power rush through the craft.

"Looks like you found the 'on' switch, Snake," said Chameleon.

"He's found more than that," added Dragon. "Look." He pointed at a screen in the middle of the control panel. It flashed with a blue glow. An image crystallized on the screen. It was an image of a half-parrot, half-chimp who was sitting in the very cockpit in which the lizards were now sitting. The Lethal Lizards watched intently as a recorded log of the ship's past played back on the monitor.

"Commander Beak recording on ship's log," said the creature on the screen. "Following Vetvix's orders to explore this planet, I have landed my craft. I am preparing to step out and begin recording the life I discover here."

The Lethal Lizards watched the screen in amazement as Commander Beak stepped from the ship. Almost instantly, he was attacked by a horde of hungry crocodiles. Though he fought fiercely, the half-parrot, half-chimp was no match for the carnivorous crocs. He was swiftly torn to shreds. Then the recording ended and the image on the viewscreen turned to static.

"So this ship belongs to someone named Vetvix," said Chameleon. "Who is this Vetvix?"

"Maybe the ship can tell us," said Dragon. Over the next few hours, Dragon studied the ship's computer. Viewing the ship's past logs, he learned of Vetvix and her plan to conquer the universe. Chameleon watched what Dragon was doing with one eye while his other eye looked around the ship. Snake fell fast asleep.

Finally, Dragon learned about Emperor Jon and how he ruled the universe with kindness and fairness. "What gives that wimp the right to rule?" hissed Dragon, a small lick of flame shooting from his mouth in a rage. "*We* are all-powerful."

"Yeah!" said Snake from the rear of the ship, now wide-awake after a full nap.

"We — rather, *I* — should rule the universe," continued Dragon, getting more and more excited at the thought.

Chameleon gave him a nasty look.

"With your help, of course," said Dragon, looking at the others.

Chameleon grunted and turned away.

"The one bit of information I can't find out from this ship is where this Emperor Jon lives," Dragon continued. "However, his trusting and loyal subjects should be able to provide us with this fact . . . with a little persuasion, that is — Lethal Lizard style! Let's get this ship moving! We've got a universe to conquer!"

"Wait!" shouted Snake. "Before we go, we need to come up with a name for our ship."

"A name?" asked Chameleon, each of his eyes rolling in a different direction.

Dragon thought for a moment. "I christen this ship the *Rapacious Reptile*!" he said at last.

"That's great! That's fabulous! I love it!" said Snake. "I only have one tiny question. What's 'rapacious' mean?"

"It means 'hungry for power,'" explained Dragon.

"That's us!" said Snake. "Let's get out of here."

Dragon pressed a sequence of buttons on the control panel and the sleek, silver ship streaked into the sky. Within minutes, the Lethal Lizards had rocketed away from Reptilius and were swiftly speeding through the jeweled blackness of space.

Dragon and Chameleon examined the star charts on the ship's console, trying to navigate the *Rapacious Reptile*.

"You're going the wrong way!" Chameleon sneered at Dragon, who was piloting the spacecraft.

"Nonsense!" snapped Dragon in his usual arrogant tone. "I am not now, and am never, wrong. We are looking for the nearest inhabited planet. And according to these charts, that would be the planet Klod. It should be appearing out that window, right about . . . now!"

A beautiful blue-green world rose into view out the front window of the *Rapacious Reptile*.

"So you were right, Boss," said Snake.

Chameleon rotated one eye to glare at Snake, or at least as much of a glare as he could manage with one eye. With his other eye, Chameleon focused on the ship's controls, assisting Dragon in putting the craft into orbit around Klod. The planet now filled the window before them.

"What a beautiful world," said Dragon snidely. "It's a pity we have to crush it!" Then he hissed a wicked laugh. Small sparks of flame escaped from his mouth as he cackled. "Prepare for landing!"

The *Rapacious Reptile* skidded to a stop on the surface of Klod with a loud roar and a dull crunch of metal. Dragon's enhanced brain was able to figure out how to pilot the ship, but there was no substitute for practice when it came to smooth landings.

"Nice landing, Boss," Chameleon said sarcastically. *I knew I should have been the pilot*, he thought.

"Look's like someone's noticed us, Boss," said Snake, peering out the window at a battalion of human soldiers who quickly surrounded the ship, weapons drawn.

It was not often that a ship landed on Klod unannounced, and it was even rarer that the landing was as rough and sloppy as the one Dragon

32

had just made. The planet's first line of defense had responded instantly.

"Attention, alien ship," boomed a voice from a loudspeaker. "Come out with your hands over your heads."

Dragon threw open the ship's hatch. His huge bulk squeezed through the opening. "Some of us don't have hands," he told the soldiers. "Just claws."

Snake popped his head out. "Yeah, and some of us don't even have those!" he added.

A panicky murmur rippled through the group of soldiers. "Giant, talking reptiles," the soldiers muttered to one another.

The three Lethal Lizards shot forward with astonishing speed. Before the startled soldiers knew what hit them, the deadly beasts tore into the troops. Dragon slashed two soldiers, one with each front leg, while he launched a stream of fire from his mouth that smothered four members of the Klod imperial guard. He ripped a tree out by its roots and swung it like a club, wiping out six more soldiers in the process.

Snake bit a soldier with his venomous fangs. The soldier fell to the ground, twitching. Two soldiers tried to approach Snake from behind. "Sneaking up on Snake, eh?" he snarled. He coiled his sinuous body around the two soldiers and squeezed until they passed out.

One soldier slipped behind a tree and took careful aim at Dragon with his weapon. "I've got you now," he muttered to himself.

"Wait!" called another soldier. "Help!" The first soldier glanced down and saw the other soldier lying wounded on the ground. He lowered his weapon and rushed to his friend's side.

"Are you all right?" asked the first soldier, kneeling down.

"Never better," said his friend, rising to his feet and transforming back into Chameleon. He stunned the soldier with his tongue and ran over to join the others, thinking, *I'm getting good at this transformation thing!*

The Lethal Lizards had devastated the best troops on the planet. When the destruction was almost complete, Dragon grabbed the last soldier by the throat and lifted him up over his head. "Where is the leader of this planet?" Dragon hissed.

The soldier grunted and wheezed, then pointed to a large building on a hill that appeared to be several miles away.

Dragon tossed the soldier aside like a rag doll. "There!" He pointed at the building the soldier had indicated. His body surged with the feeling of his power. "We will destroy that place next and learn the location of Emperor Jon from the leader within."

"If you kill everyone in the place, we'll never learn a thing," said Chameleon. "I've got a better plan. Just listen!"

Dragon snorted a breath of fire from his nose. He hated to admit when Chameleon was right, but he controlled his temper and listened to the plan.

A few minutes later, a human dressed in royal robes appeared at the front door to the governor's mansion. Word of the lizards' attack had not yet reached the governor.

"I am Noel Emahc," said the stranger, "royal assistant to Emperor Jon. I must speak to the governor at once."

The two guards nodded and led the man to the governor's office.

"Delighted to meet you, Assistant Emahc. I am Klutz, governor of Klod," said the governor, extending his hand in greeting. Emahc stared at Governor Klutz's outstretched hand, then slowly raised his own. The governor grabbed it and shook it heartily. "So, how is my old friend, the emperor?" asked Klutz, glancing up at a framed photograph on the wall. The picture showed the governor shaking hands with a goofy-looking man in a striped shirt, checked polyester pants, a long robe, and a crown.

"Oh, just fine — swell, as a matter of fact," replied Emahc uneasily.

"And how are things on Polyester?" Klutz inquired. "What brings you here?"

"Actually, your first question answers the second," Emahc replied cryptically. "So it's time for me to leave." He turned and headed for the door.

"But you just got here," complained the governor. "You must stay for lunch. I insist."

Suddenly, a long reptilian tail sprang from the back of Emahc's robes. *Oh, nuts!* thought Noel Emahc (*Chameleon* spelled backward). *I thought*

I could hold this form longer! It seems certain shapes are harder to hold than others.

"What is this?" asked Klutz in shock.

Just then, two of the governor's guards burst into the office. "Sir, we've just received word of an attack by three huge, superpowered reptiles."

His secret revealed, Chameleon changed completely into his reptile form. "Actually," he sneered, "we prefer to be called the Lethal Lizards." He fired his tongue at the governor, who dropped to the floor, stunned. Then he lashed out with his tail at the two guards who charged him. He knocked them over like bowling pins.

Chameleon dashed from the governor's mansion and soon rejoined the others. "Let's get out of here!" he shouted. "I know where the emperor is. And I know what he looks like!"

Dragon piloted the ship back into space.

"Set your course for the planet Polyester," instructed Chameleon. "Home of Emperor Jon!"

The *Rapacious Reptile* blasted into lightspeed, on its way to the planet Polyester so the Lethal Lizards could continue their assault on Emperor Jon's universe.

6

In the emperor's palace on Polyester, Sorcerer Binky had fallen into a deep sleep. Things had been pretty boring around the palace, and Binky now dozed on the emperor's special vinyl-upholstered, reclining lounge-chair throne.

He drifted into a dream in which he was the most powerful sorcerer in the universe. He strolled through a beautiful forest, with magical power radiating from his fingertips. Trees lifted their roots from the ground and strolled alongside him. Mountains bellowed their greetings as he passed, and all the creatures of the forest gathered around him. Binky waved his hands like a conductor and led the animals in a glorious symphony of sound, but then he noticed one of the animals making an urgent, beeping noise.

"Hey!" he shouted in the dream. "Someone's off-key around here."

The beeping grew louder and louder. Sorcerer Binky woke from his dream with a start, to discover that he had fallen off the reclining throne onto the linoleum throne-room floor. The beeping continued. "Ah, just as I was about to find my true calling as a symphony conductor," Binky muttered, picking himself up. "What's that beeping? It's driving me nuts."

Binky glanced at the throne-room control panel and saw a signal light flashing in time with the beeping. "Uh-oh," said Binky. "That's no off-key singer. That's an incoming message on Emperor Jon's emergency frequency!" Binky flipped a switch and a disturbing image filled the viewscreen.

On the screen, the face of Governor Klutz of the planet Klod was still dazed from the recent attack by Chameleon. "I must speak to Emperor Jon at once," said the governor in a raspy, strained voice. "Something terrible has happened."

Oh, boy! Sorcerer Binky thought to himself. "Your governor-ship, I have some bad news myself," Binky said. "Emperor Jon is currently away on vacation."

"Well, three giant, superpowered lizards just trashed my planet," explained Governor Klutz. "They call themselves the Lethal Lizards."

"That's terrible!" replied Binky.

"But that's not the worst part!" the governor continued.

"Not the worst part!" exclaimed Binky. "What could be worse? Did they forget to leave a tip? I know I hate it when people do that. I imagine it's even worse when large, superpowered lizards do it."

"No," said Klutz. "What's worse is the reason they attacked my planet, which was to find out where Emperor Jon lives. At this very moment, they are on their way to Polyester!"

"On their way to Polyester? Is that all?" replied Binky. "I thought it was something serious, like — Holy cow! *I'm* on Polyester!" shouted Binky, the realization of what Governor Klutz had said finally sinking in. "That means they are headed here!"

"At least the emperor will be safe," said Klutz. "But what will you do?"

"There's only one thing I *can* do," replied Sorcerer Binky. He dashed to a corner behind the throne and dragged a heavy, black cauldron into the center of the room. "I've got to place an emergency call to the only ones who can help us: *Pet Force!*"

Our universe, WackyWorld theme park . . .

"I read about this ride when I looked up Wacky-World on the Internet," said Jon Arbuckle. Jon, Garfield, Pooky, Odie, Arlene, and Nermal were standing in front of Wendell Wacky's Tunnel of Terror. "It's a really scary haunted-house boat ride."

"What do I need to see a haunted house for?"

Garfield said to the others. "I live with Jon. After about a month of dirty laundry building up, his house is scary enough."

The gang piled into a boat and floated toward the tunnel entrance, a gaping opening in the shape of a monster's mouth. "This is nothing," Garfield continued, groaning and complaining as he rolled his bulk around the boat. "I've been close to Jon's mouth when it's been open. I can't imagine anything more terrifying than his breath."

"Here we go! It's time to be scared!" said Jon in a spooky voice.

"No," muttered Garfield. "Missing a meal — now that's scary. This — this is just dumb."

The boat slipped into the monster's mouth and plunged into total darkness. They couldn't even see their own noses, so Jon had no idea that Garfield, Arlene, Pooky, Odie, and Nermal had suddenly disappeared!

Emperor Jon's universe, the emperor's throne room . . .

FLASH! Garzooka, Starlena, Compooky, Odious, and Abnermal emerged through Sorcerer Binky's bubbling cauldron and stood, stunned, in Emperor Jon's throne room.

"Oh, please," whined Garzooka. "Not again. I thought we were done with this suffering superhero stuff."

"Oh-boy-oh-boy-oh-boy!" shrieked Abnermal in an ultra-annoying voice. "I'm Abnermal!"

"You're telling me," said Garzooka. "Abnermal, abnormal, same in any universe!"

"Sorcerer Binky, I don't see Emperor Jon," said Starlena, looking around the throne room. "Where is he?"

"I'm Abnermal!" Abnermal shouted again, firing off a freeze blast just for the fun of it. He accidentally encased the sorcerer in a block of ice. "And Pet Force is back!"

Odious looked at the frozen form of Sorcerer Binky. He licked the sorcerer's icy shoe and his tongue — super-stretchy stun tongue though it was — immediately stuck to the ice.

"Yeah, we're back, all right," said Garzooka dryly. "And better than ever."

"My analysis indicates that something is very wrong," announced Compooky. "I am amazed at the fact that Sorcerer Binky could bring us here from our universe without the use of the cover of *Pet Force #100*, the usual doorway between dimensions. Where is Emperor Jon? And why did the sorcerer bring us here?"

"He's the only one who can tell us," said Starlena, pointing at the Binky Popsicle.

"Great," muttered Garzooka. "And Annoying Lad here went and froze him. I could try melting him with a gamma-radiated hairball."

"I'm concerned that the radiation might harm Sorcerer Binky," said Compooky.

"I was talking about Abnermal," replied Garzooka, giving his pint-sized partner a grumpy look.

"Really funny, Garzooka," replied Abnermal, glaring back at the Pet Force leader. "We could wait for the ice to melt."

"But there's no food here!" shouted Garzooka, his fist shooting out and sending Abnermal flying through the air.

Compooky jetted over to the sorcerer's cauldron. "Perhaps this bubbling liquid will do the trick," suggested Compooky.

"Binky's magical brew?" asked Starlena, the concern showing in her voice.

"It is created from his own magic," said Compooky. "Therefore he should be safe."

"What about the genius's tongue?" asked Garzooka, indicating Odious. The clueless canine rotated his head from side to side, his eyes crossing as he stared at his tongue. The tongue was still frozen to the sorcerer's shoe.

"Let's begin there," said Compooky. He directed Starlena to pick up a long-handled ladle, scoop a cup of bubbling brew from the cauldron, and pour a bit of it onto the spot where Odious's tongue met the ice. The murky brown liquid blurped and bubbled, sending a column of steam into the air. Within seconds, Odious was free.

However, Binky's brew had magically transformed Odious's tongue into a long, flat lasagna noodle.

Garzooka's eyes widened. He licked his lips.

"Don't even think of it!" said Starlena sternly.

Odious's tongue then changed into a piece of rope, a telephone wire, and the sole of a boot before changing back into his own slobbering tongue.

Compooky poured a larger cupful of magical brew over the block of ice that encased Binky. The brew bubbled, the ice melted, and Sorcerer Binky transformed into a six-foot-tall maple tree.

This time it was Odious's eyes that widened. He headed straight for the tree.

7

Before Odious reached the tree-form of Binky, the sorcerer changed several more times. The tree became a jukebox, blasting out hit tunes that Abnermal proceeded to dance to. Then the jukebox turned into a lounge chair, which Garzooka sat on, stretching all four of his limbs. Finally, the sorcerer changed back into himself, standing up and sending Garzooka sprawling onto the floor.

"Hey!" shouted Sorcerer Binky. "What's the big idea? I bring Pet Force here because the emperor's universe is in grave danger, and you guys freeze me, then go play with my magical brew! You think it's fun being a jukebox?"

"You did play some great songs, you have to admit," said Abnermal. Garzooka sent Abnermal flying across the room again. Odious trotted over and slobbered on Abnermal's head.

First smart thing that dog has done all day, thought Garzooka. *Make that all year.*

"What's the grave danger that caused you to

bring us here?" asked Garzooka, stepping into his role as leader of the team.

"And how did you bring us through the dimensional portal when we were so far away from the *Pet Force #100* cover?" added Compooky.

"I was able to find you in that amusement park by scanning your universe through my cauldron," Sorcerer Binky explained to Compooky. "I had a clear reading of all five of you, so I was able to use the cauldron alone to pull you through. I'm getting better at the whole dimensional-transporting routine." A big smile crossed the sorcerer's face, his mind temporarily stuck on the glory of his magical achievement.

"Um, Sorcerer Binky," said Starlena gently. "The danger? The reason you brought us here?"

"Oh, yeah," said the sorcerer, focusing on the matter at hand. "Emperor Jon is away on vacation on the amusement planet Funlandia."

"I wonder if it's as much fun as WackyWorld," said Abnermal, who had snuck back to the front of the group. Garzooka once again sent him soaring across the room.

"At this very moment, three superpowered creatures known as the Lethal Lizards are on their way here!" the sorcerer explained. "I got an emergency call from the governor of a planet they've already destroyed. I need you, Pet Force. Emperor Jon needs you."

"We should contact the emperor. He needs to know about this extreme situation — he could be at risk!" said Garzooka.

"I didn't want to disturb him on his vacation," said Sorcerer Binky. "But I think you're right, Garzooka. This is an emergency that threatens our entire universe."

Sorcerer Binky dashed over to the throne-room communications panel and sent an emergency signal to Funlandia.

"Funlandia! The land of fundia! Ha-ha!" said a cheerful operator who received the call. The operator was wearing glasses with eyeballs that bounced on springs, a beanie with a propeller, and a bow tie that spun around as he talked. "If you'd like a brochure showing all the fun things to do on Funlandia, press 1."

"Actually," began the sorcerer, "this is an emer —"

"Uh-uh," interrupted the operator. "You haven't heard all the options yet. If you want a guided virtual tour of the planet, press —"

"LISTEN!" shouted Sorcerer Binky, using his incredibly loud voice. He had learned to control his super-loud voice and could call on it when needed. "I don't want a brochure! I don't want a tour! I need to speak with Emperor Jon, who is on vacation there. I'm calling from his palace with an emergency that affects the entire universe!"

"Well, that doesn't sound like fun," said the operator.

"IT'S NOT FUN! IT'S AN EMERGENCY!" shouted Binky.

"Still, are you sure you don't want a brochure?" asked the operator. "They're quite attractive."

"No brochure," growled the sorcerer, magical steam spouting from his ears. "Just get me the emperor!"

"Could you please spell that for me?" asked the operator.

"IT'S EMPEROR JON, THE RULER OF OUR UNIVERSE!" exploded Binky.

"Well, why didn't you say so?" replied the operator. "I'll locate him and call you back." The monitor went dark.

"Now that's a guy who knows what fun is," said Abnermal.

"I can see why Emperor Jon would go to a place like that," muttered Garzooka. "He'd look good in one of those beanie caps."

Sorcerer Binky paced back and forth across the throne room. A few minutes later, the communications console beeped. Binky rushed to it and saw the face of the operator on the screen.

"It's Funlandia, the land of fundia, with your call," said the operator in his happy singsong voice. "Hold for Emperor Jon."

The screen went dark for a few seconds, then the image of Emperor Jon appeared. He was wearing bouncing eyeball glasses, a propeller beanie, and a spinning bow tie, just like the operator. "Having a great time! Wish you were here!" said the emperor. "But why did you call me away? I was just watching the finals of a turtle race. Each race takes a day and a half to complete, you know. I can hardly stand the excitement."

"Sounds like great fun," said Garzooka. "Love your outfit." What he was thinking was, *Only someone like Emperor Jon, who considers boredom a hobby, would enjoy a race that takes a day and half!*

"Garzooka! Pet Force! What are you doing there?" asked the emperor, noticing the heroes standing next to Sorcerer Binky.

The panicked sorcerer quickly filled the emperor in on the destruction on the planet Klod and the impending attack on Polyester by the Lethal Lizards.

"This is just terrible," said the emperor, the eyes on his glasses bobbing up and down. "This is awful. This is much worse than not seeing the end of the turtle race. I'll return to Polyester at once. I can't be off having a vacation while my entire universe is threatened."

"Emperor Jon," said Starlena, stepping up to the monitor. "Perhaps it would be wiser for you to stay where you are. If there is an attack on the palace here on Polyester, at least you will be safe. Protecting you has got to be our first priority."

Actually, lunch has got to be our first priority, thought Garzooka. But he kept the thought to himself.

"Good idea," said the emperor, his bow tie spinning. "Thank you, Pet Force. Once again, the safety of my universe is in your hands. Plus, this way I'll be able to catch the end of the turtle race. Only seven more hours to go. Good luck, Pet Force." Then the bouncing, spinning image of Emperor Jon disappeared.

"What do I do now?" asked Sorcerer Binky in a panic. "We've got these crazy lizards coming here. I'm no military strategist. I flunked 'Defending a Planet' in sorcerer's school — though I did get an A in 'Running and Hiding.' Will you defend the palace for me?"

"I've got a better idea," said Garzooka. "Why don't we get some lunch? I'm starving."

"Garzooka!" screamed Starlena.

"All right! All right!" said Garzooka. "Saving the universe first, lunch second. Sorcerer Binky, I think that Pet Force should take the *Lightspeed Lasagna* and try to intercept the Lethal Lizards before they get to Polyester. If we can stop them in space, then we can save Polyester from being attacked."

Compooky jetted over to the sorcerer. "I suggest that you increase security around the palace, just to be on the safe side," said the part-teddy bear, part-computer.

Sorcerer Binky nodded. "I'll signal Emperor Jon's soldiers right away," he said. "Good luck, Pet Force."

Garzooka, Compooky, Odious, Starlena, and Abnermal raced from the throne room. "Are you sure we don't have time for lunch?" asked Garzooka as Pet Force reached the garage on the lowest level of the palace where their spaceship, the *Lightspeed Lasagna*, was kept. The others scowled at him as they boarded their ship.

Back in the throne room, Sorcerer Binky sent out a signal to Emperor Jon's soldiers. Then he rested his head in his hands and moaned, "Why didn't I listen to my mother when she told me to become a teacher?"

8

The *Lightspeed Lasagna* sped through space, its five crew members hard at work. Even Garzooka was concentrating on the task at hand. What he didn't tell his teammates was that he had just secretly gobbled down an entire frozen lasagna he had stashed in the ship's freezer the last time he had appeared as Garzooka. Even as Garfield, without any superpowers, he could make a lasagna — frozen or not — disappear faster than the eye could perceive.

"I've got the course set for the planet Klod," said Abnermal, his fingers flying furiously over the ship's navigational keyboard. "Most direct route. Unless they take some long way to Polyester, we should meet up with them between here and there."

"I doubt that a gang of vicious, evil invaders with their icy hearts set on taking over the universe would waste any time on their journey," said

Garzooka, looking away from the others as he spoke so that no one would catch a whiff of frozen lasagna on his still-spicy breath.

"I've set the ship's scanners to search for reptilian life signs," announced Compooky, whose soft, furry face was buried in the scanner readouts.

"I'm tracking all spaceship activity within a hundred-thousand-mile radius of the *Lightspeed Lasagna*," added Starlena. "No one's going to slip past us."

Odious kept busy during the flight by flicking the reading lamp in the back of the ship on and off. He was shocked but thrilled each time the light came on.

"That'll keep him busy all day," said Abnermal. Then a wicked smile crossed his face as he remembered an old, favorite joke of his. "Hey, Garzooka!" he called out.

"You don't have to yell. I'm sitting right next to you," said the Pet Force leader. "Though I wish I weren't," he added under his breath.

"Hey, Garzooka," Abnermal said again. "How do you keep a moron busy all day?"

Great time for jokes! thought Garzooka, though he decided to humor his teammate. "I don't know, Abnermal. How?"

"How do you keep a moron busy all day?" Abnermal asked again.

"I don't know, how?" Garzooka once again replied.

"How do you keep —"

"I get it! I get it!" Garzooka shouted directly in Abnermal's face.

"Hey! No fair!" sniveled Abnermal, his super-feline pester-power reaching cosmic proportions. "I smell lasagna on your breath! You had lunch! What was it, that secret lasagna you stashed away last time we were in this universe?"

"You knew about that?" gasped Garzooka, trying hard to sound like the injured party.

Starlena sighed and rolled her eyes. "We all knew about that, Garzooka!" she explained. "The only thing harder for you to hide than your food is your stomach!"

The intense bickering continued until Compooky interrupted, blurting out, "I'm getting massive reptilian readings about five thousand miles ahead of us. I'm also picking up a ship at about the same distance."

Pet Force snapped back into action.

"Based on these readings," Compooky continued, "that ship is filled either with thousands of tiny lizards, or else three really big ones."

"See if you can get them on visual and try to contact them," ordered Garzooka.

Abnermal adjusted the controls on the communications panel and a faint image slowly came into view on the monitor. "I've got something!" announced Abnermal.

"You mean besides the most annoying voice in the universe?" asked Garzooka.

"Take a look," replied Abnermal, his voice now barely a whisper. On the monitor, the terrifying image of Chameleon, Snake, and Dragon came sharply into view. The three Lethal Lizards were hissing and snarling, crammed into the tiny ship they had named the *Rapacious Reptile*.

On board the *Reptile*, the image of Garzooka and Abnermal in the *Lightspeed Lasagna* filled the ship's viewscreen. The Lethal Lizards stared at the screen, then looked at one another and burst out laughing.

"What are you looking at, pussycat?" Dragon asked Garzooka.

"Pussycat?" howled Snake, letting out a roar of laughter. "Pussycat! Did you hear that one, Chameleon? Pussycat!" Snake poked Chameleon in the ribs with his fangs.

"Yeah, I heard it!" roared Chameleon, shoving Snake's head away.

"Good one, Boss," said Snake.

"Shut up, Snake!" snarled Dragon, without taking his eyes off the screen.

"Sure, Boss," replied Snake.

"Your spaceship seems to be in my way, pussycat," Dragon hissed at Garzooka. "I suggest you move it, or I'll have to move it for you."

The fur on the back of Garzooka's neck bristled.

"He's huge!" whispered Abnermal, intimidated by the sight.

"I'd say he's about twice as massive as an average Komodo dragon," explained Compooky.

"Quiet, Pet Force," Garzooka said tersely. His teeth were clenched firmly, his eyes were narrowed into tightly focused beams, and his stomach grumbled as it worked overtime on the frozen lasagna. "I am Garzooka, leader of Pet Force," he said calmly to the snarling image on the monitor. "We defend this universe from all evil-doers. I warn you not to underestimate our powers."

"Uh-oh, the pussycat gave us a warning, Boss," said Snake on board the *Rapacious Reptile*. "We'd be quaking in our boots, if we had any boots!" The three lizards burst out laughing again.

"You still haven't considered my suggestion, pussycat," hissed Dragon, a small lick of flame escaping from between his huge teeth. "Will you move your ship, or do I have to move it for you?"

"I think it's time to show these laughing lizards just who they're dealing with," Garzooka said to his teammates back on the *Lightspeed Lasagna*. "End communication."

The viewscreens on both ships went black. The two vessels were now within several hundred yards of each other.

"Abnermal, extend your force field around the *Lightspeed Lasagna*," ordered Garzooka. His fur still stood on end. Odious came over and found a glob of cheese from a pizza Garfield had eaten two weeks earlier hidden under the upright fur. Odious licked the cheese off and trotted away. "Compooky, power up main weapons," Garzooka continued. "Everybody prepare for battle!"

Pet Force moved into action like a finely tuned machine. While Compooky got the *Lightspeed Lasagna*'s weapons ready, Abnermal reached out with his protective force field and surrounded the ship in preparation for weapons fire from the lizards. Starlena focused the ship's sensors on the *Rapacious Reptile* to give Garzooka his best chance of targeting the enemy ship. Odious sniffed the back of Garzooka's neck, hoping to find more cheese.

"Keep them lined up in the targeting sights," ordered Garzooka.

"Got 'em!" shouted Starlena. "They're coming into weapons range . . . *now!*"

"Here we go," said the Pet Force leader. Shafts of flaming laser fire blazed from the *Lightspeed Lasagna*, striking the *Rapacious Reptile* and sending the ship spinning out of control. "Direct hit!" exclaimed Starlena.

On board the *Rapacious Reptile*, the three Lethal Lizards toppled over one another as their ship rotated like a top.

"We're hit!" shouted an alarmed Snake. "It's all over! Our glorious reign of evil ended by a pussycat. A pussycat with some serious weapons!"

"Stop panicking," ordered Dragon, who was furiously trying to stop the ship from spinning. "We've got to regain control."

"I've got an idea," said Chameleon. "Switch control to me."

"Why?" snarled Dragon, who never liked to give up any power.

"Because my eyes can rotate in sync with the ship," explained Chameleon. "I've got a better chance of stabilizing us."

"Go!" yelled Dragon, switching power to Chameleon's copilot seat.

"Yeah, and do it fast, because I'm getting really dizzy," said Snake, whose head spun around and around with the ship.

Chameleon's huge eyes began to rotate. Within a few seconds, his eyeballs were spinning in exactly the same motion as the ship. To him, the control panel appeared to stop moving. Chameleon adjusted the ship's guidance system and the *Rapacious Reptile* stopped spinning. "Now let's hit back!" snarled Chameleon, powering up the ship's weapons.

The *Rapacious Reptile* fired off round after round of deadly proton pulses — energy blasts that could tear a ship apart. Each one exploded on the shield Abnermal had placed around the *Lightspeed Lasagna*, rocking the Pet Force ship.

"I can't hold the shield any longer," said Abnermal to his crewmates. "I'm going to have to let go!"

"My analysis indicates that the proton pulses are draining Abnermal's life energy," reported Compooky.

"Can we work it so that they just drain his pester-power?" asked Garzooka.

"I'm afraid not," replied Compooky. "He must release the shield."

"Let go!" ordered Garzooka. "I'm going to hit them with a full barrage and make the shield unnecessary!"

Abnermal released his force field and slumped back in his seat. Garzooka fired the full force of the *Lightspeed Lasagna*'s weapons in a searing burst. Blazing beams of laser fire shot toward the *Rapacious Reptile*.

At the same moment, Chameleon fired a series of proton pulses. The two barrages collided in space, setting off a massive energy shock wave that rocked both vessels. The *Lightspeed Lasagna* and the *Rapacious Reptile* both went spinning out of control, plummeting toward crash landings on a planet below.

9

"**P**ull up! Pull up!" shrieked Abnermal as the mountainous, rocky planet rushed toward the front window of the *Lightspeed Lasagna.*

"I'm trying!" shouted Garzooka. "The controls are not responding! They're sluggish!"

"Maybe you should make them a cup of coffee!" snapped back Abnermal.

"Pull up! Pull up!" shouted Dragon at that same second on board the *Rapacious Reptile* as the same craggy terrain sped toward the three lizards.

"I'm trying!" yelled Chameleon, who was still piloting the craft. "The controls are sluggish!"

"Maybe you should threaten to rip their heads off!" snarled back Dragon.

"They're responding!" cried Garzooka with relief. "We're leveling off. I can't get enough altitude to pull back into space, though. Brace yourself, Pet Force, we're going to crash!"

"I've got control!" announced Chameleon, trying to sound as if he had never been worried. "But I can't get us back up into space. We're going to crash into this planet. Hang on!"

WHOOOMP! BASH! SCREEEE!

The spaceships slammed into the rocky surface of the planet with two loud *thuds*, followed by sharp, metallic screeches as they skidded to halts within sight of one another.

"Is everyone all right?" asked Garzooka, when their stomachs had caught up to the rest of them.

"I'm fine," said Starlena. "And nice landing. I couldn't have done better myself!"

"I could have!" said Abnermal. The others glared at him. "Kidding! Just kidding! Nice job, Garzooka. I'm fine."

"I, too, am unharmed," replied Compooky. "I will begin repairs on the *Lightspeed Lasagna* at once."

Garzooka glanced to the back of the ship and saw Odious hanging from a cargo rack by one leg. He seemed perfectly happy and seemed not to notice his upside-down state. Starlena helped him down.

"If those lizards survived, they'll be looking for

a fight," said Garzooka. "And Sorcerer Binky says they are pretty powerful customers."

"We're ready," said Abnermal.

"Let's go," ordered Garzooka.

On board the *Rapacious Reptile*, the three Lethal Lizards gathered themselves after the rough landing.

"I should never have let you be pilot," Dragon snarled at Chameleon.

"If you were piloting, we'd still be spinning around and around in space," countered Chameleon.

"The only good part of this mess is that the Pet Force pussycats have also crashed on this planet," said Dragon, rising from his seat.

"Pet Fools. We will crush them swiftly," said Chameleon, joining Dragon. They both stopped at the door of the ship and looked back at Snake. He had taken the worst of the crash. His eyes now rolled around in his head, his thin tongue dangled, and drool dripped from the corner of his mouth. He looked like a very long, scaly version of Odious.

"Mommy?" Snake asked when Dragon approached for a closer look. "What time is dinner?"

"Mommy!" exclaimed Dragon. "Come on, snap out of it!" Dragon bopped Snake on the top of the head. A shudder went through his long body. Then his eyes stopped rolling and his mind came into focus.

"Hey, Boss, where are we?" Snake asked. "What's the plan?"

"Battle," replied Dragon. "That's the plan." Then the Lethal Lizards leaped from the *Rapacious Reptile*.

Garzooka spotted the lizards as soon as he stepped from the *Lightspeed Lasagna*. "I've got the dragon," he announced to his teammates, breaking into an all-out run. "Look out for the others!"

Garzooka and Dragon slammed into one another full force. "So I meet the big, bad pussycat in person," quipped Dragon as he sliced at the Pet Force leader with his supersharp claws.

Garzooka swiped right back with his razor-sharp right claw. "Time to put you into a terrarium," he said out loud. "Only I don't know of any terrariums for criminals, so a prison cell will have to do." He fired a gamma-radiated hairball at Dragon, who met the glowing, furry orb with a blast of his fire breath. The heat from the fire detonated the hairball, and the resulting explosion of gamma energy knocked both battlers to the ground.

I've never battled another superpowered being with abilities so much like mine, Garzooka thought as he struggled with Dragon. *It's almost like fighting myself — except not as handsome. I wonder if this guy likes lasagna!*

Meanwhile, Starlena focused a concentrated siren song right at Snake, who slithered toward her menacingly. But because snakes don't have ears (they hear differently than other creatures), her powerful siren song didn't affect him.

"Pretty tune," said Snake as he continued to advance on Starlena. "It's a shame no one else will hear it. Not after I'm done with you." Snake wrapped himself around Starlena with astonishing speed and squeezed tightly, choking the voice right out of her.

"Hang on, Starlena," shouted Abnermal, firing a freeze blast that encased Snake's head in a block of ice. "Take that, you blockhead!" he shouted.

Startled, Snake released Starlena, who stumbled away to catch her breath.

By this time, Dragon had scrambled back to his feet. He fired a blast of his fire breath at Snake, which quickly melted the block of ice. It also singed the skin on Snake's face, but Snake was happy for the trade-off. Dragon then turned back to his slugfest with Garzooka.

Snake turned on Abnermal. "I'll teach you to encase my head in ice," he hissed as he bared his deadly fangs.

"You don't have to teach me," declared Abnermal. "I already know how!"

Snake lunged forward, his glistening fangs headed right for Abnermal's throat.

"You also don't have to teach me to do this!" shouted Abnermal, throwing up his force shield to block the poisonous fangs.

67

Snake's face bounced off the shield. "You've got plenty of tricks, don't you, little pussycat?" he hissed. "But so have I! If I can't get through your shield, I'll take you, shield and all!" Snake's eyes narrowed and his enormous jaws opened wide, then wider and wider. With a swift gulp, he swallowed Abnermal whole!

"Garzooka!" yelled Starlena. "The snake has swallowed Abnermal whole!"

Garzooka looked over at Snake and saw the outline of Abnermal halfway down the length of the beast. Snake looked as if he were two parts snake and one part scaly version of Abnermal.

"We've got to get him out!" shouted Starlena.

"We do?" asked Garzooka, fending off a punch in his continuing battle with Dragon. He returned a superpowerful strike to the midsection of the Lethal Lizards' leader.

"Garzooka!" yelled back Starlena. "This is no time for jokes!"

"Who's joking?" replied Garzooka, ducking to avoid another deadly blow from Dragon. "Besides, I'm a little busy here!"

"No problem," replied Starlena. "My voice has recovered enough from that big squeeze to do a little damage." She focused a burst of siren song right at Dragon, who reeled backward from the impact, stunned.

As Dragon struggled to keep standing, Garzooka dashed over to Snake. Snake's ferocious fangs grew down from his upper jaw, and those fangs were aimed right at Garzooka. The Pet Force leader grabbed one fang in each hand, then stepped on Snake's lower jaw with his feet. Pressing down with his legs and lifting up with his arms, using the fangs like handles, Garzooka pried open Snake's huge mouth.

"Slide on out of there, Abnermal!" Garzooka shouted into Snake's mouth.

"It's kind of nice in here, actually," came the reply, echoing from Snake's belly. "Except for the clammy, squishy, damp darkness, of course. And the smell! Phew! I don't know what this guy eats, but he could use a couple hundred breath mints right here in his stomach."

"Now, Abnermal!" shouted Garzooka, laboring to keep the struggling Snake's jaws wide open. "I can't hold this forever!"

Chameleon saw what was happening and fired his dynamic, darting tongue at Garzooka, hoping to distract him. But Odious came to his teammate's defense, countering swiftly by firing his own super-stretchy stun tongue. Odious's tongue clashed with Chameleon's tongue in midair. The two tongues entwined and their force sent Chameleon and Odious spinning around and around until they both went flying. They landed in a twisted heap, their tongues finally untwirling.

Inside Snake, Abnermal generated a thin sheet of ice leading from the creature's belly right out through his mouth. He then dove headfirst and slid his way out, crashing into Garzooka when he emerged. This sent both heroes flying as Snake's mouth slammed shut.

Suddenly, Compooky came rushing over to Garzooka. "Garzooka, we just got an emergency message from Emperor Jon!" Compooky announced. "He must speak with you at once!"

"What?" said a startled Garzooka. "Why is he calling us here?"

"It doesn't make any sense!" added Starlena.

This slight distraction was all the Lethal Lizards needed. They struck swiftly. Dragon, now recovered from the siren song, landed a crushing blow to Garzooka's jaw. Snake wrapped himself around Starlena and quickly squeezed until she passed out. Then Dragon fired a blast of fire at Abnermal, who resisted it as long as he could with his shield, but soon passed out from the strain as well.

Odious looked from Dragon to Snake to Compooky. The utterly clueless canine watched as Compooky began to change form. Within seconds, he had shifted into his true form — that of Chameleon!

The always-baffled Odious was even more confused upon seeing this sight. Chameleon fired his dynamic, darting tongue, knocking Odious into a heap with his unconscious teammates.

"Nice trick, Chameleon," said Dragon. "Why'd you wait so long?"

"I noticed you couldn't finish off the pussycat without my help," countered Chameleon.

Dragon grumbled, shoving Chameleon aside and heading back to the *Rapacious Reptile*.

"Those guys were tougher than we thought," said Snake to Chameleon. "And the little guy tasted real bad!" The two joined their leader in the ship.

The *Rapacious Reptile* had sustained only minor damage, so it didn't take the Lethal Lizards very long to make their needed repairs and take off, heading once again for Polyester.

"This time there'll be no one to stop us!" snarled Dragon as the *Rapacious Reptile* sped through space.

10

When the real Compooky emerged from the *Lightspeed Lasagna* to inform his teammates that his repairs to the ship were complete, he was shocked to discover the others sprawled across the ground, unconscious.

"Obviously the battle did not go too well," Compooky said to himself. He sent a small electric shock from his computer power source into Odious's brain. The tiny electric charge somehow worked its way into Odious's dream. In the dream, he was endlessly chasing his tail around and around in a circle, slobbering the whole time, creating a moat around his body. But he stopped short when a tiny image of Compooky floated up to him and called out his name.

Odious woke to find Compooky floating before him with his teammates lying unconscious on the ground. Odious stood over Abnermal and slobbered onto his face. The *drip, drip, drip* woke up Abnermal. "What happened to us?" he asked.

"It appears that the Lethal Lizards got the better of you this round," responded Compooky. "We'd better wake the others."

Abnermal fired a mild cold burst at Starlena. It acted like a splash of water in her face and she jumped to her feet, startled but fully conscious. "It all happened so quickly," she said to Compooky. "You came out of the ship to tell us that Emperor Jon had called, and the next thing I knew, *wham*! We were all out."

"But I didn't come out of the ship," explained a puzzled Compooky. "There was no message from Emperor Jon. I just came out now and found you all in this condition."

"But if it wasn't you . . ." began Starlena.

"Apparently, Chameleon is true to his name," concluded Compooky. "It seems he can take on the appearance of others. In this case, me!"

"We've got to follow them before they destroy all of Polyester," exclaimed Abnermal. He turned and started toward the *Lightspeed Lasagna*.

"Aren't you forgetting something?" asked Starlena, motioning toward the unconscious form of Garzooka.

Abnermal looked around and shrugged. "No, nothing I can think of."

"Abnermal!" shouted Starlena. "What about Garzooka?"

"He's fine just the way he is."

"He is our leader, after all," said Starlena. "Now give me a hand waking him up."

Abnermal dashed to Garzooka's side. He started poking, prodding, and kicking the Pet Force leader, his pester-power reaching cosmic proportions. "Get up, come on, you lazy fat cat, get up. I have a nice, hot, steaming pan of lasagna here, but I'm going to eat it all. That's right, none for you. So *get up!*"

Abnermal's pester-power finally did the trick. Garzooka eyes popped open. Then his right arm shot out in a fist, sending Abnermal flying all the way back to the ship.

"What happened?" Garzooka asked, getting to his feet.

Compooky and Starlena filled him in as Pet Force sped to the *Lightspeed Lasagna*. "We've got to stop them," said Garzooka, his head beginning to clear. "Or it's the end of Emperor Jon's universe!"

"Well, duh!" said Abnermal, climbing into the ship. Then the *Lightspeed Lasagna* took off in hot pursuit of the *Rapacious Reptile*.

"I want this to be quick and easy," announced Dragon as the *Rapacious Reptile* entered orbit around the planet Polyester.

"Without those pussycats around, it should be a piece of cake," said Snake.

"Let's just go in, grab the emperor, and get out," said Chameleon. "We can negotiate his release and state our demands from the safety of a hidden planet."

"How will we find him?" asked Snake.

"Using the readings from this ship's computer, I've set our scanners to search for his life signs," explained Dragon.

"Well, what are you waiting for?" asked Chameleon. "Flip it on and let's find the guy!"

Dragon snarled and hissed a small lick of flame toward Chameleon as if to say, *Don't make me remind you who's boss!* Then he engaged the ship's scanners. After a few minutes, a scowl crossed his face. "There's no sign of the emperor anywhere on this planet!" he growled.

"Are you sure?" rumbled Chameleon.

"Look for yourself," snarled Dragon.

Chameleon scanned the entire planet, but found no sign of Emperor Jon. "I have found the location of the emperor's palace," said Chameleon. "Let's begin our attack there. Someone in the palace must know where the emperor is!"

The *Rapacious Reptile* swooped down toward Emperor Jon's palace on Polyester. Sorcerer Binky had placed troops around the palace just in case Pet Force failed in their attempt to stop the Lethal Lizards. Looking out the throne-room window, the sorcerer was horrified to see his worst nightmare coming true.

The lizards opened fire on the troops, blasting them with proton pulses. The soldiers fired back with laser rifles, but they were no match for the power and speed of the streaking spacecraft. The *Rapacious Reptile* landed right in front of the palace's main gate. The Lethal Lizards sprang from their ship and charged at the last group of soldiers defending the palace.

One soldier aimed his laser weapon at Dragon, who grabbed it in his powerful claws before the soldier could fire. "Stand aside or die!" shouted the leader of the Lethal Lizards as he crushed the barrel of the rifle, then bent the entire weapon in half. He tossed it aside.

"I will defend this palace with my life!" stated the soldier calmly.

"Yes, you will," hissed Dragon. He swiped at the soldier with his nasty claws.

Snake slithered over to a group of three soldiers. Before they could fire their weapons, he wrapped himself around one, bit the second with his poisonous fangs, and then swallowed the third soldier whole. The last remaining palace troops fought bravely, but it was an exhausting struggle against the thick-skinned Lethal Lizards.

In the emperor's throne room, Sorcerer Binky cringed behind a chair. "Where is Pet Force?" the sorcerer wondered. "Were they so easily defeated by these supersized lizards? Is there no hope for us? And why am I talking to myself?"

Suddenly, a knock came at the throne-room door. Sorcerer Binky cowered in fear. "Go away!" he shouted.

"But it's me," said a muffled voice from the other side of the door. "I'm back."

"Emperor Jon?" whispered Binky in astonishment. He raced to the door and flung it open. There stood Emperor Jon, complete with long, flowing robes, golden crown, white vinyl belt, and polyester pants. "Why are you back, Your Royalness?" the sorcerer asked in amazement. "I thought we agreed it was best that you stay away!"

"Changed my mind," Emperor Jon said tersely. "Couldn't leave the palace empty."

"Well, it's not exactly empty," responded Binky, slightly annoyed at the insult.

"I cannot turn away from my duty as leader of this universe," stated Emperor Jon. "We must find a way to stop these lizards."

"I summoned Pet Force, Your Emperorness," explained Binky. "They took off in the *Lightspeed Lasagna* to intercept the lizards before they reached Polyester, but obviously they were not successful!"

"Well, then it's a good thing I rushed back so quickly," said the emperor.

Sorcerer Binky stared at the emperor. "How *did* you get back here from Funlandia so quickly?"

he asked. "And what made you change your mind about staying away?"

"I wouldn't want to miss the destruction of this planet," snarled Emperor Jon — only it was not Emperor Jon! The form of Emperor Jon started to change. Within seconds, Chameleon stood towering over Sorcerer Binky. "Now that I've found out what I've come for, we'll be taking off — for Funlandia!"

Without warning, Chameleon fired his dynamic, darting tongue, striking Sorcerer Binky who then crashed to the floor, out cold.

Chameleon was startled by the roar of spaceship engines. He dashed to the throne-room window and saw the *Lightspeed Lasagna* landing in the middle of the battle that still raged outside. He

sprinted from the throne room and raced down the palace stairs.

In front of the palace, Pet Force jumped from their ship and raced into battle. "This time, the ending will be different, Dragon," shouted Garzooka as the two leaders grappled in a match of superstrength against superstrength.

"Aw, I hate it when someone tells me the ending, pussycat," replied Dragon, struggling to get the upper hand — or in his case, upper claw — on Garzooka. As he and Garzooka struggled, Dragon opened his mouth to blast the Pet Force leader with his fire breath, but Abnermal leaped onto Garzooka's shoulders and fired a freeze blast right down Dragon's throat, neutralizing his fire breath briefly.

"Chill out, Dragon," joked Abnermal. "I just love saying that!"

"Normally I'd slug you for using that horrible pun for the millionth time," said Garzooka as Dragon stood stunned by the freeze blast. "But I've got my hands full now. And thanks."

Snake immediately slithered over to Odious, wrapped himself around the clueless canine, and began to squeeze. Odious struggled with all his strength to keep from being crushed. He tried to fire his super-stretchy stun tongue at Snake's head, but he couldn't muster the energy to lash out with his wily weapon.

Chameleon burst from the front gate of the

palace. Seeing that Snake had things well in hand — so to speak — he rushed to Dragon's side and grabbed Garzooka's right arm to give his boss an advantage.

Two on one is definitely not fair, Starlena thought. She quietly approached Chameleon from behind, but she hadn't counted on the superb seeing ability of his independently rotating eyes. While his right eye remained focused on aiding Dragon, Chameleon's left eye whirled around and spotted Starlena.

"It's not nice to sneak up on people," Chameleon said to Starlena, who was directly behind him. Starlena stopped in her tracks just as Chameleon turned his head and fired his dynamic, darting tongue at her, knocking her away.

But while Chameleon had his efforts focused on Starlena, Garzooka wrestled his arm from Chameleon's grasp. Garzooka lashed out with that arm and threw the shape-shifting lizard twenty feet away. Garzooka then brought his razor-sharp right claw down toward Dragon, who grabbed Garzooka's wrist just in time to save his thick-skinned throat. The evenly matched battle of behemoths continued.

Starlena recovered from Chameleon's darting tongue and saw that Odious was just about out of strength and breath in his struggle to keep Snake from squeezing the life out of him. Starlena raced to his aid, but Snake saw her coming.

"I'm in the mood for a bite," hissed Snake. He struck quickly, sinking his fangs into Starlena's arm and shooting his venom into her bloodstream. Her eyes rolled up and she passed out, collapsing to the ground.

During the split second it took Snake to bite Starlena, he loosened his grip on Odious slightly. Odious took advantage and, gathering all his remaining strength, pushed his way free of Snake's suffocating squeeze. He fired his super-stretchy stun tongue, striking Snake in the head. This sent Snake slithering away, twitching and groaning.

Odious sprang to Starlena's side, where Abnermal was already trying to revive her.

Dragon broke free from Garzooka's grip, but instead of rushing into another attack, he turned and ran toward the *Rapacious Reptile*, where Snake and Chameleon had already gathered. In a flash, the Lethal Lizards boarded their ship and blasted off the surface of Polyester. They disappeared into the cloudy sky above.

Garzooka signaled Compooky, then hurried to Starlena's side. Compooky raced from the *Lightspeed Lasagna* to join the others huddled around the unconscious form of Starlena.

Compooky quickly analyzed the situation. "Snake's poison is flowing through her blood," he announced after doing several rapid tests. "I'm afraid she only has a few minutes to live!"

11

Garzooka and Abnermal frantically paced back and forth in front of the unconscious Starlena. Her skin had turned a sickly shade of green. Compooky searched the memory banks of his supercomputer brain, desperately looking for a solution. Odious knelt next to Starlena, looking at her curiously and drooling an ever-widening puddle next to her head.

"There's got to be something we can do to save her!" cried Garzooka. "Look at her! She's the same color as cheese mold. It's a disgrace!"

"We need some way to draw the poison out of her system," stated Compooky.

It was then that Garzooka noticed the huge puddle of drool Odious was creating next to Starlena. "Odious, will you stop it?" said Garzooka. "Your drool is enough to drown Starlena — as if the poison weren't enough."

"That's it!" exclaimed Compooky. "Odious's slobber power is tremendous. If we could find a way to reverse it, maybe he could suck the poison from Starlena's system."

"How do we do that?" asked Abnermal.

"Oh, what a headache I've got!" groaned a voice from behind Pet Force. The four heroes turned to see Sorcerer Binky stumble from the palace. "That Chameleon guy hit me with his tongue," complained Binky. "It really knocked me for a loop. It's almost as strong as when Emperor Jon takes off his shoes. What took you guys so long anyway?"

"Never mind that," replied Garzooka. "We need your help. Starlena's been bitten by Snake, and she only has a few minutes before his venom does her in. We need you to create a spell to reverse Odious's slobber power so he can suck the poison out of her system. Can you do it?"

"Right after I conjure up something to get rid of this headache," muttered the sorcerer.

"*Now!*" shouted Garzooka.

"All right! All right! Just don't yell. It makes my head hurt worse," moaned Binky. He pulled a pocket-sized book of spells from his robe. "Now let's see," he said, flipping through the pages. "*Reboot . . . revenge . . .* here we go, *reversals.*"

Binky closed his eyes and concentrated hard. Then he began to chant, "Evil forces, now we clobber, reverse this puppy's power of slobber!"

A bright light flashed, then suddenly Odious's drool stopped. He leaned down and licked

Starlena's arm, right where Snake had bitten her. The poison leaped from her body, drawn out of the bite wound by the tongue's slobber power. As the poison left her system, the green color of her skin faded away and her normal color returned.

Sorcerer Binky chanted again, "Reverse again this brainless fool, let him resume his life of drool!" Again a bright light flashed. This time, the poison poured from Odious's mouth, forming a large, green puddle that smoked and bubbled, then disappeared.

Starlena moaned and stirred, then opened her eyes. "What happened?" she asked softly. Garzooka explained as he helped her to her feet.

"Where'd the lizards go?" Starlena asked.

"I don't know," replied Garzooka. "They ran to their ship and took off."

"I think I can answer that one," said Sorcerer Binky. "Chameleon came to me, appearing as Emperor Jon. He tricked me into revealing where the real emperor is. The Lethal Lizards now know that Emperor Jon is on Funlandia. I'm afraid they're headed there to capture him and claim control of the universe."

"Are you up for another fight?" Garzooka asked Starlena.

"I'm ready," she replied, feeling stronger each second.

"Then let's go to Funlandia and finish this thing!" snarled Garzooka. "To the *Lightspeed*

Lasagna!" Then Garzooka and his teammates ran to their ship and took off in hot pursuit of the Lethal Lizards.

"Good luck, Pet Force," Sorcerer Binky muttered as he flipped through his book of spells. "Let's see, *headquarters . . . headlights . . .* oh, here it is, *headaches*!"

12

The Lethal Lizards struck the planet Funlandia with savage fury. Being a vacation and amusement planet, Funlandia had no defenses, since it never feared attack. The *Rapacious Reptile*'s proton pulses leveled hotels and restaurants, destroyed beaches, and terrorized the fun-seeking tourists who made up most of the planet's population.

After their opening calling card of destruction, the Lethal Lizards landed the *Rapacious Reptile* near the office of the governor of Funlandia. The governor was much more of an administrator — running the vast amusement planet — than he was a political leader. He stepped from his office, followed by his assistants, just as the lizards emerged from their ship.

The governor was dressed in large, baggy clown pants, a striped shirt, and suspenders. He wore a beanie cap with a propeller on top — the official hat of Funlandia — and a big, red clown's nose. "I don't understand all this violence!" said the governor. "I'm sure we could have given you three some kind of discount or group rate, if money was an issue. We accommodate beings from over 500 different worlds. Certainly we could have worked something out."

"Money is not the issue," hissed Dragon. Then he let loose with a blast of fire breath, burning the governor's office to the ground. "Taking control of this entire universe is the issue."

"Oh, well," stammered the governor in shock as he watched his office burn. "I'm afraid I can't help you there. None of our vacation packages include control of the entire universe. You'll have to speak to Emperor Jon about that one."

"That's precisely why we are here!" snarled Dragon. "Tell us where we can find the emperor!"

"He's probably in his palace on Polyester," replied the governor with his fingers crossed. "Where else would he be?"

Dragon turned and aimed a blast of fire breath at the governor's car, burning it to a crisp. Then he grabbed the governor by the suspenders and lifted him high into the air, sending his red nose flying. "You're a bad liar," said Dragon. "I happen to know that the emperor is on this planet. And if I know it, then you must know it, too. Now tell me where he is, or I fry *you* next!"

"Okay! Okay!" yelped the governor. "I liked that car. And the nose, too!"

"The emperor!" shouted Dragon.

"All right," replied the governor. "Emperor Jon is in the main amusement park, about fifty miles north of here. You can't miss it. It's got the biggest roller coaster in the universe."

Dragon tossed the governor aside like a used gum wrapper and stomped back to the *Rapacious Reptile,* followed by his teammates. Within seconds, they were airborne and zooming toward the amusement park.

"There it is!" shouted Chameleon as the huge roller coaster came into view. Surrounding the roller coaster were other rides and midways filled with happy vacationers having fun. "Scanning for the emperor's life signs," Chameleon added. "Got him! There!" He pointed down at a kiddie ride made up of small cars attached to spokes that spun around and around on a track. The ride looked like a giant wagon wheel with a car at the end of each spoke. These were not "drive-it-yourself" cars. The rider simply sat in the seat and was spun around by the ride. In one of the tiny seats sat Emperor Jon.

The *Rapacious Reptile* came tearing down toward the ride at scorching speed with its weapons blazing. A proton pulse struck the ride, ripping it from its base. The ride, along with several children and Emperor Jon, went spinning off like a top.

"Whoa!" shouted Emperor Jon as the normally sedate ride spun off faster and faster, sailing through the air. "This ride is a lot more exciting than it looks!" The ride climbed hundreds of feet into the air, above the crowded park, then came shooting down, plummeting toward the ground.

"I don't think it's supposed to work like this!" said the emperor, finally catching on as the ground and crowd rushed toward him at frightening speed.

Suddenly, a spaceship roared into view. Emperor Jon recognized the *Lightspeed Lasagna* as it swooped down below the plunging ride and landed.

Garzooka, Odious, Starlena, and Abnermal stormed from the ship into the wagon-wheel-like shadow cast by the falling ride. "Stand strong!" Garzooka shouted to Odious. Then the Pet Force leader leaped onto Odious's shoulders. The clueless canine set his legs firmly, then grabbed Garzooka's ankles. "Steady," called Garzooka. "Here it comes!"

Garzooka reached up with his powerful arms and caught the spinning circular ride, preventing it from crashing to the ground. Both Garzooka and Odious strained from the impact of stopping the plunging ride, but the mighty muscles of Pet Force held, and soon Emperor Jon and the children were safely off the ride.

"Pet Force," said the emperor, shocked but pleased to see the superheroes there, in the middle of his vacation. "What are you doing here?"

"They're here to protect you from us," hissed a voice from behind the emperor.

Emperor Jon spun around and saw the three Lethal Lizards approaching menacingly. "Those lizards!" he exclaimed. "The ones Binky told me about! They're here!"

"We intend to take you with us," snarled Dragon.

"And we intend to stop you," replied Garzooka. "This ends here and now!"

"My thoughts exactly, pussycat!" spat back Dragon.

Before anyone could move, the *Lightspeed Lasagna* suddenly lifted off, flying just above the heads of the superpowered beings gathered below. Compooky, who was piloting the ship, grabbed Emperor Jon with a tractor beam, pulled him up into the ship, and sped off, taking the emperor safely away from the scene of the impending battle.

"Nice move, Compooky," said Garzooka under his breath. "At least Emperor Jon is safe for now."

"Should we get to the ship and follow them, Boss?" asked Snake.

"No," replied Dragon "Once we finish off these four, there will be no one to stop us from getting the emperor!" Then Dragon let loose a stream of fire breath right at Pet Force.

As the terrified vacationers of Funlandia fled for cover, Abnermal threw up a wall of ice that met the torrent of fire head-on, blocking the deadly flames.

Odious leaped onto Snake's head, covering his eyes. "Hey, get off me, you dumb mutt! I can't see!" screamed Snake. He thrashed about like a bucking bronco, whipping Odious from side to side.

Dragon slammed into Garzooka and the two superstrong adversaries went flying right into the amusement park's midway. "Can't get enough of me, huh?" quipped Garzooka as the powerful pair destroyed booth after booth. They emerged on the other side of the midway, covered in stuffed animal prizes and soaked to the bone from the Dunk-a-Clown booth. They rolled over and over on the ground in a titanic battle of strength. Garzooka kept one fist tightly over Dragon's mouth to prevent his fire breath from instantly ending the battle.

Chameleon lashed out at Starlena with his tongue, but Abnermal blocked the blow with his force shield. He then fired a freeze blast at Chameleon, which encased him in a solid block of ice.

"That's one down," said Abnermal. "Let's go give Odious a hand."

But inside the block of ice, Chameleon went through a transformation. He changed his shape, expanding into a great whale, whose giant form shattered the frosty cage. Enraged, he transformed back and fired his tongue at Abnermal and Starlena, sending the two Pet Force heroes flying through the air. They crashed through the roof of a nearby building, landing inside the Funhouse of Mirrors. Chameleon followed them inside.

"Hey, look at me! I'm tall!" said Abnermal, peering at a seven-foot-tall version of himself in one of the mirrors. He thought he was talking to Starlena, but the form of Starlena suddenly changed into that of Chameleon. The lizard stunned Abnermal with his tongue. The pint-sized, pestering member of Pet Force passed out.

Chameleon turned a corner and found himself face-to-face with Starlena. "Your turn, songbird," he hissed. He fired his tongue at her, but it was merely her reflection in a funhouse mirror. Chameleon's tongue shattered the mirror into a thousand tiny fragments.

"Two can play the illusion game, at least in here," said Starlena from behind Chameleon. Before the Lethal Lizard could spin around, Starlena fired a concentrated siren blast right at him. Chameleon fell unconscious to the floor.

Starlena rushed to Abnermal's side. He was just coming around. "Is it over, Starlena?" he asked. "Did we win?"

"Come on," she said, ignoring his question. "Help me get Chameleon outside."

Abnermal and Starlena each grabbed one of Chameleon's legs and dragged his inert form from the funhouse.

Meanwhile, Odious refused to let go of Snake's head. Thrash as he might, Snake could not shake the powerful grip of Odious, who finally managed to plant his hind legs on the ground. Shifting his weight, Odious lifted Snake into the air.

"Oh, no," cried Snake. "I'm afraid of heights!"

Odious spun around and around, maintaining his firm grip on Snake's head. The rest of Snake's body swung in a circle like a giant whip. When he

had picked up enough speed, Odious let go. Snake went soaring through the air, wiggling like a worm, going higher and higher until he landed in the front car sitting at the very top of the biggest roller coaster in the universe.

"Good idea!" shouted Abnermal as he and Starlena reached Odious with the limp, unconscious body of Chameleon. "Bet you can't make that shot again."

Odious took the challenge literally. He grabbed Chameleon by the ankles and spun around and around once again, releasing Chameleon and sending him up to join Snake in the car at the top of the roller coaster.

This did not go unnoticed by Dragon as he struggled with Garzooka. Dragon managed to kick Garzooka away, then sprinted to the roller coaster to help his teammates.

Dragon climbed up the roller coaster track. "I will rescue my backup troops, and then we will all deal with you, pussycat," hissed Dragon as he scurried up the track.

"I have a better idea," declared Garzooka, climbing up the track behind him in hot pursuit. "I'll stop the three of you right now!"

As he neared the top of the roller coaster, Dragon turned and let loose a blast of fire breath over his shoulder.

Garzooka flattened himself against the tracks. The stream of fire passed just inches above his head. Garzooka got up and spat a series of gamma-radiated hairballs at Dragon, who was approaching the roller coaster cars from behind and had just reached the rear car near the top of the track.

Blam! Blam! Blam! The hairballs exploded as they hit. The force of the blasts sent him flying through the first six cars. He landed in the front car, behind Chameleon and Snake, just as they regained consciousness.

The impact of Dragon's landing moved the front car forward along the peak of the track ever so slightly. Gravity did the rest. The Lethal Lizards went zooming down the track, gaining speed as they went.

"Yikes! How do you get out of this thing?" shouted Snake in absolute fear.

"You don't! You want to jump?" asked Dragon. "You'll be crushed like a worm. No offense."

"Well, you're our so-called 'boss'! What's your plan?" snarled Chameleon.

Dragon had no answer. The car raced forward, with the lizards too afraid to look.

Starlena sped into action. She floated up to the level of the speeding car and let loose with her siren song. The meow that wows stunned Dragon and Chameleon. The two large lizards collapsed right onto Snake, knocking him out, too.

The rushing roller coaster car reached the bottom of the descent and crashed into the safety barrier at the very end of the track. The car splintered into pieces, and the momentum sent the three lizards tumbling over one another. They landed in a heap on the ground. Abnermal was waiting.

"Three frozen lizard-pops coming right up," he announced. Then he froze the Lethal Lizards in a thick cage of ice. "Though I have to admit I like orange, strawberry, and grape a lot better."

Garzooka climbed down the roller coaster track and was soon reunited with the others. "I'll send a signal to Compooky to bring Emperor Jon back," explained Garzooka. "Then we'll call law officers to come cart these three away for a long time!"

Compooky returned with the *Lightspeed Lasagna*. A short while later, a large transport ship arrived carrying three lizard-proof cages. The unconscious bodies of the Lethal Lizards were loaded into the cages, then placed on board the transport ship, which took off on the long journey to the penal planet.

"I told you all along *I* should have been boss," hissed Chameleon through the bars of his cage after the lizards had regained consciousness.

"Am I going to have to spend the rest of my life listening to you whine?" snarled Dragon.

"Yeah, I think so, Boss," said Snake.

"Shut up, Snake!" shouted Dragon.

Pet Force boarded the *Lightspeed Lasagna*. Emperor Jon stayed on board, deciding to catch a ride home with the heroes.

"I liked my vacation on Funlandia," said the emperor when the ship had blasted into space. "I think I'll go back next year. The rides there are more exciting than I had counted on. Especially that last one with the lizards!" The members of Pet Force nodded at one another. *Same old Jon*, thought Garzooka. They settled in for the trip back to Polyester.

Once back at the palace, Sorcerer Binky wasted no time in sending the five furry heroes back through the portal to their own universe.

"Thank you once again, Pet Force," said Emperor Jon, just before they disappeared. "I hope we don't need your services again for a very long time."

"Nice vacation, huh?" asked Sorcerer Binky sarcastically.

"Wonderful," replied the emperor, missing the sarcasm completely. "They had this one ride with lizards. It was a little scary, but very exciting. Let me tell you about it."

Sorcerer Binky rolled his eyes and sat back to listen to the emperor's tale.

13

Our universe, WackyWorld theme park . . .

*Z*AP! Garfield, Arlene, Pooky, Nermal, and Odie reappeared in the boat next to Jon Arbuckle. They were in the pitch-black Tunnel of Terror in the WackyWorld theme park. In this universe, only a split second had passed since they had disappeared and experienced their entire Lethal Lizards adventure as Pet Force. Spooky sounds filled the darkness. A green, ghostly face lit up, then went dark.

"Pretty cheesy," said Garfield. "And speaking of cheese, once again, I'm starving! All this superhero, saving-the-universe stuff works up quite an appetite."

"For you, blinking works up quite an appetite," replied Arlene.

The boat emerged from the darkness of the haunted house into the bright daylight.

"Well, that wasn't very scary," complained Jon. "I thought we'd have a great adventure or something, but that was pretty tame."

The others all looked at one another. *If he only knew*, thought Garfield. *Now when's lunch?*

Epilogue

The transport ship carrying the caged Lethal Lizards glided silently through the blackness of space. It was headed for the penal planet where the three superpowered lizards of the universe would be locked up for a very long time.

"Ready to go to light speed," announced the ship's first mate.

"Let's do it," replied the captain. With the flip of a switch, the huge transport ship slammed into light speed and disappeared from view.

What the captain didn't know was that just as the ship went into light speed, it happened to be passing by the *Floating Fortress of Fear*, secret hideout of Vetvix, the evil veterinarian. The ship created a spatial shock wave when it hit light speed. The force was like a giant wave of energy, and it collided with the *Fortress*. The huge space station rocked back and forth violently, shaking everything on board.

In her laboratory, deep in the fortress, Vetvix — whose head was attached to the body of a lizard — watched from her force field prison as the *Fortress* shook. Vetvix looked on wide-eyed with excitement as a large book of magical spells fell from a bookcase. The massive, leather-bound volume landed on the lab's control panel. And as luck would have it for Vetvix, the huge book landed right on the on/off switch of the force field prison that had held her since Pet Force had trapped her there.

As the book hit the on/off switch, the force field shut off. "I'm free!" shrieked Vetvix with glee. She scampered around the lab on her lizard feet. "I must find the rest of me!"

Vetvix raced through the *Fortress* until she found the cow that had her arms, the gerbil that had her legs, and the cheetah whose head was connected to her body. With great effort, she herded the mutant creatures to her lab, then guided them into her combination machine. She powered up the machine, pushed a sequence of buttons on the control panel, dashed into the combination chamber, and waited as lights flashed and power surged through her ghastly device.

The various pieces of Vetvix broke apart from the animals to which they were attached and slowly floated toward one another. Within minutes, her arms, legs, head, and body were all reacquainted. Vetvix was re-formed, and evil power rushed through every cell of her body once again.

Vetvix stepped from the machine and switched it off.